ROYAL TREATMENT

SUDDENLY
ROYAL

ROYAL TREATMENT

K. R. COLEMAN

MINNEAPOLIS

Darby Creek
A division of Lerner Publishing Group, Inc.
241 First Avenue North
Minneapolis, MN 55401 USA

For reading levels and more information, look up this title at
www.lernerbooks.com.

Cover and interior images: Igor Klimov/Shutterstock.com (background texture); GoMixer/Shutterstock.com (coat of arms and lion); KazanovskyAndrey/iStock/Getty Images Plus (gold); mona redshinestudio/Shutterstock.com (crown).

Main body text set in Janson Text LT Std 12/17.5.
Typeface provided by Adobe Systems.

Library of Congress Cataloging-in-Publication Data

Names: Coleman, K. R., author.
Title: Royal treatment / K.R. Coleman.
Description: Minneapolis : Darby Creek, [2019] | Series: Suddenly royal | Summary:
  Grace Valmont-Diaz is an unpopular sixteen-year-old, who dreams of escaping
  small-town Iowa. But when she learns of her royal heritage and receives a warm—
  but possible insincere—welcome in her homeland, Evonia, she must decide if she
  really wants her title and all it entails.
Identifiers: LCCN 2017053158 (print) | LCCN 2017061160 (ebook) |
  ISBN 9781541525986 (eb pdf) | ISBN 9781541525726 (lb : alk. paper) |
  ISBN 9781541526419 (pb : alk. paper)
Subjects: | CYAC: Identity—Fiction. | Secrets—Fiction. | Nobility—Fiction. | Social
  classes—Fiction.
Classification: LCC PZ7.1.C644 (ebook) | LCC PZ7.1.C644 Roy 2019 (print) | DDC
  [Fic]—dc23

LC record available at https://lccn.loc.gov/2017053158

Manufactured in the United States of America
1-44556-35487-2/28/2018

To Aiden, my amazing niece
who has always loved to read

The Valmont Family of Evonia

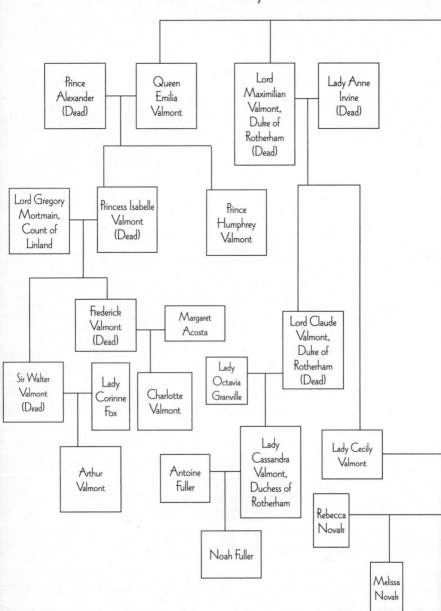

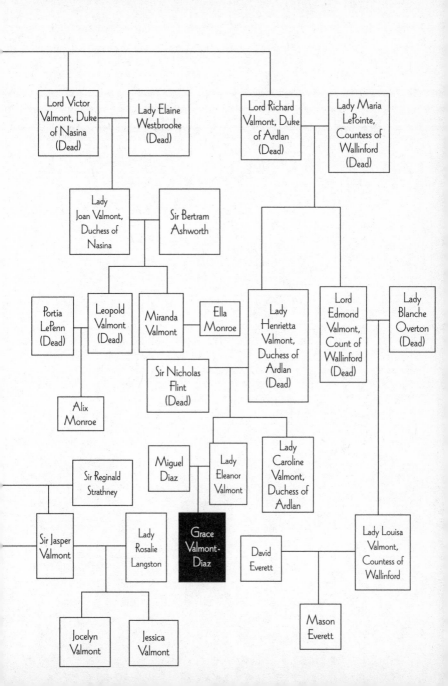

1

The summer I turned sixteen seemed to stretch before me like the endless cornfields that surrounded my hometown of Colton, Iowa. I was bored. I was restless. And thanks to my parents' recent divorce, I no longer had a permanent home. Instead I was stuck rolling back and forth between my parents' places on my skateboard.

I found myself wishing that at least one of my parents had moved somewhere more interesting after the split.

Even though we'd lived in Colton my whole life, I'd never felt like any of us belonged in this town. My mom is from the European country of Evonia, and although she moved to America ages ago, she still didn't seem to be fully comfortable in Iowa. She is a respected art history teacher at a small liberal arts university but doesn't do much socializing outside of work. And my dad is a former *almost* rock star who is still more concerned with making music than getting to know the neighbors. Although this left me with far more knowledge about frescoes than the average teenager, plus some reasonably impressive skills with a guitar, it didn't exactly pave the way for community involvement. Or for me to hang out with the neighborhood kids.

The handful of friends I have were away at summer camps or on family vacations, leaving me to fend for myself.

So there I was. Skating down the sidewalk from my dad's house to my mom's. A new song my dad and I had been working on was rolling around in my head. I was so focused on the chords that I jumped in surprise when a car horn blared behind me.

I turned around and saw Chrissy Swenson, captain of the soccer team, the most popular girl in my grade, and perpetual thorn in my side, driving her black jeep. There were four other girls from the soccer team riding along.

Chrissy grinned at me as she slowed to cruise along at my speed. "Hey look, guys, it's Grace," she said. "And she's added some blue streaks to her hair. Isn't she cool? Don't you want to be just like her?"

"I bet the color washes out," the girl sitting closest to me in the back seat said. And before I knew what was happening, she stood up and reached her water bottle out the window. A blast of cold water hit the side of my face.

I lost my balance and had to jump off my skateboard before I fell off.

As I stood dripping, I could hear the girls laughing.

"She has the least amount of grace I've ever seen in my entire life," Chrissy said in a voice loud enough for me to hear as they drove away.

I wiped away the water drops streaking down my face and thought about how much I wanted to get out of Colton.

2

I rolled up to my mom's house and let myself in. Several things immediately surprised me. First, my mom was wearing a nice dress instead of jeans and a T-shirt like she usually wore.

And second, she was cleaning. Or, more accurately, she was running around the living room throwing random things into a laundry basket. My mom rarely cleaned. Usually books and papers were scattered everywhere. She always had at least three projects going on at the same time, but cleaning was never one of them.

"Grace!" she said in surprise as I came in. "You're here."

"It's your week to have me," I said. "Lucky you." This had become a pretty typical exchange over the last few months. My mom usually didn't keep track of when I would be coming and going.

"I just thought you wouldn't be here until later."

Just then, the front door opened again and my dad stepped into the house.

"I came as soon as I got your text," he burst out.

"Grace is already here too," my mom said, giving him a pointed look.

I looked at my mom and then at my dad. "What is going on?"

"Why don't you sit down," my mom said, pointing to a comfy blue chair.

I sat, and my parents sat down across from me on a cat-hair-covered couch.

"We have something to tell you," my mom said, looking nervously at my father. "My sister is in the States and she wants to meet you."

I looked at her confused.

"Wait. What? You have a *sister*?" I was shocked. I had always assumed my mom was an only child, just like my dad. The only thing she ever told me about her family back in Evonia was that her had parents died when I was little. She never mentioned a sister.

"Why didn't you tell me?" I didn't know what questions to ask first. I had an aunt! "What's her name?"

"Caroline," my mom said. "She'll be here this afternoon."

I sat there, stunned.

"And I was always going to tell you," my mom said. "It just never felt like the right time."

"You couldn't find the right time to tell me that you had a *sister*? That I had an *aunt*?"

"It's complicated," my dad jumped to my mom's defense.

That was exactly what they'd said when I'd asked why they were getting a divorce. The fiery ball that had lived in the pit of my stomach since the divorce blazed up, hotter than ever. "Well, don't bother trying to explain then," I said coldly. "When I meet Caroline, I can ask her."

"Actually," said my mom hesitantly, "I'm not sure if it's a good idea for you to meet her."

"What?"

"I just don't know if now is the right time for her to come into your life."

"You didn't seem to think about timing with anything else you've thrown at me this year. As far as I'm concerned now is the perfect time," I snapped. "Maybe it means I can find some family that I can actually rely on."

I didn't even let the accusation sink in before I grabbed my skateboard and stormed out of the house, letting the screen door slam behind me.

3

Once I'd stormed out, I wasn't sure where
to go. I realized I had no idea when my aunt
was getting here—Mom had just said "this
afternoon"—and I didn't want to miss her
arrival. But I couldn't just sit on my mom's
front steps for hours either. It was way too
hot to be outside for that. I decided to go
to the corner convenience store to bask in
their air conditioning and grab a slushie.
Maybe that would help me calm down.

I rolled down the street, thinking, *An aunt.
How much does she know about me? And why don't
I know anything about her?* I felt blindsided.

Within ten minutes, I'd gotten to the store,
bought myself a cherry slushie, and began

skating slowly back toward my mom's house. Sipping on my drink, I started coming up with my plan of attack. I had more questions to ask. More things I wanted to know. Things I *deserved* to know.

As I approached my mom's house, I saw that a spotless black SUV had pulled up along the curb right outside. My heart sped up. *Could this be—*

Behind me, an engine revved. I looked back, worried it might be Chrissy and her friends again, but it was just an old pickup truck instead.

By the time I turned to face forward again, it was too late. I was only feet away from the SUV. A man in a black suit was holding the door open for a woman in a cream-colored dress who was stepping out right in front of me. I tried to swerve but lost my balance. The cherry slushie flew into the air and hit the ground like a grenade. For the second time that day, I flew off my skateboard. This time I landed hard on the sidewalk. When I looked up, I saw red slushie splattered all over the woman's cream dress and satin shoes. I groaned at the sight of it.

"Miss? Are you all right?" the man in the black suit asked, helping me stand up.

"I'm so sorry. I didn't see you," I said to the woman as she tried to wipe the slushie off her dress.

She mumbled something about American carelessness. And then she pointed down to my skinned knee. "Duncan," she said to the man in the black suit. "She needs to be taken care of. She seems to be injured."

"I'm fine," I said.

The man in the suit took a handkerchief from his pocket and handed it to me.

"Put pressure on it," he said. As I did, I looked up at the woman again and realized she had the same amber-colored eyes as my mother and me.

"Caroline?" I guessed.

"This is Lady Caroline Valmont, Duchess of Ardlan," Duncan said in a firm tone.

"Oh. Uh, sorry, I thought you were my aunt."

The woman did a double take. "Is your mother Eleanor?"

"Yes," I said. "And I'm Grace."

We each stood there frozen, looking at each other.

4

After staring at me for a long moment, my aunt said, "What is that in your nose?"

"A nose ring," I said.

She looked slightly horrified. "Your mother let you put that there?"

"She's not a fan of it," I admitted. "But she's always encouraged me to develop my own style."

"I see," Caroline said.

"So," I said, trying to change the subject, "how did you get to be a duchess?"

Her eyes widened. "Has your mother told you nothing?"

"Well, I just learned I had an aunt about thirty minutes ago," I said.

She grew silent. Her lips pursed. And then she took my hand in hers.

"Grace, darling," she said, "there is so much you don't know. Where do I even begin?"

"What do you mean?" I asked.

"Your mother and father didn't leave Evonia on good terms."

"They never told me that."

"Yes, well, there was a bit of a . . . disagreement within the family," Caroline said slowly. "And we've been out of touch for too long. But I'm here to put an end to that. I want to get to know my only niece. Make amends. Heal our family."

I could tell that there was more to this story, but I was grateful and a bit relieved that *she*, at least, was willing to open up to me.

I smiled at her hesitantly.

"Can I call you Aunt Caroline? Or do I have to call you Lady Caroline whatever-it-was that Duncan called you?" I asked.

My aunt gave me a genuine smile. "Aunt Caroline would be perfect."

At that moment, my mom and dad

came out onto the porch.

"Caroline," my mom said, eyeing my aunt's red-stained dress.

"Eleanor," Caroline said in a clipped voice as my mom approached. They learned in and kissed each other twice on each cheek, but their tones were icy.

And then my mom saw me.

"Grace!" she said, surprised. "You're back." She looked me up and down and spotted my skinned knee. "Are you okay?"

"Yeah, I'll be fine, but I think I might have ruined Caroline's dress. I should take her inside so she can change."

Duncan grabbed a small suitcase out of the back of the car, and he trailed behind my aunt as she followed me inside. My dad tried to say something to Caroline, but she walked past him as if he didn't exist. I saw him look back at my mom and my mom shake her head. Whatever happened years ago, I could tell that nobody was over it.

I took Aunt Caroline upstairs to the spare bedroom that used to be my dad's old office.

"Do you want me to get you some stain spray?" I asked as Duncan set her suitcase on the bed.

"No thank you, dear," she said. "I'm not sure if this poor dress can be saved."

"There's a dry cleaner down the street. I can run it there," I offered.

"I will take care of it," Duncan said to me. "Why don't you go make your aunt some tea?"

"Uh, sure."

When I entered the kitchen, my mom already had the teakettle on the stove.

"There's some iced tea in the fridge," I said, realizing how warm the house was already.

"She'd never drink iced tea," my mom said dismissively as she searched through the tins of tea in the cupboard.

"Mom," I said. "Did you know Caroline is a duchess?"

My mom's hand froze in midair. Her back stiffened. She slowly turned around to face me.

"Why don't the three of us sit outside on the porch," she said as my dad walked into the kitchen. "It's getting hot in here."

I followed them out on the porch and slumped down in a wicker chair.

"So," I said, "what's the deal with your sister being a duchess?"

My mom looked at my dad and took a deep breath. "My sister and I belong to Evonia's royal family, the Valmonts."

"Did you say *royal* family?" Without even giving her a chance to answer, I burst out, "Why am I only hearing about all this now?"

My mom dropped her gaze. "I didn't want to burden you with my past," she said. I watched as my dad reached for her hand.

"Tell me everything." I stared at my parents' hands.

"Well, your great-great-great-grandfather was King of Evonia many years ago," my mom began.

"A king?"

"Yes," my mom said, her eyes looking sad.

"So," I asked. "Does that make me a princess?"

My mom hesitated. "Not exactly, but it does make you royal."

The teakettle whistled inside. None of us made a move for it. I heard the click of Duncan's shoes cross the kitchen tiling and the whistling stopped. The silence felt louder than the kettle had been.

"So I'm royalty," I finally said, testing out the sentence.

"You are," my aunt said, stepping onto the porch. "And someday you will inherit my title and become a duchess too."

5

My aunt sat down in the wicker chair next to
mine, and Duncan appeared with a tray of tea.
He passed around hideous mugs my mom had
gotten from an overly eager student—the only
matching set my parents owned, as far as I
was aware.

My parents and aunt sat quietly. But I
wasn't going to let my parents get away with
this so easily. The anger that had subsided in
the shock of meeting my aunt had started to
bubble up again.

"So." I fixed my mom with an accusatory
glance. "What else have you been keeping
from me? Is there more I should know?"

My parents were both silent.

"Would you like me to tell her?" Aunt Caroline asked.

My mom shot her a look that did nothing to hide her anger. "*We* will tell her."

"Fine." My aunt sat back in her chair again.

"Your father and I met in Evonia," my mom began, glancing over at my dad.

"I know," I said impatiently. "Dad was traveling around Europe trying to make it big with his band, and you worked at an art gallery. I've heard this story before."

"Yes," my mom said. "We fell in love fairly fast."

"Too fast, in some people's opinion," my dad added, glaring at my aunt.

"So I brought your dad home to meet my family."

"And the family was not impressed," Aunt Caroline said before she took another sip of tea.

"It was not their decision to make," my mom fired at her sister. "And not up to the family to pass judgement. Instead of supporting my marriage to Miguel, you all told me to break it off."

Aunt Caroline's calm demeanor slipped away. "I just wanted you to be happy. And now look, you're divorced. You could've saved yourself years of heartache. It was such a mistake."

"Please, Caroline," my mom hissed at her sister. "It was not a mistake. My beautiful daughter was born because of that marriage."

For the first time since she'd arrived, my aunt looked ashamed.

"Of course," Caroline said, looking first at my mom and then at me. "I didn't mean that. I was so happy the day you were born, Grace. I was one of the first ones to hold you."

"You were there?" I said, surprised. "You came all the way to the States?"

There was a strange silence again.

"You weren't born in America," my mom said shortly. "You were born in Evonia."

"I was what?" I practically jumped out of my seat. My parents had kept so much from me. This was the last straw.

"Grace, please," my dad said. "Let us finish the story."

"No. I want Caroline to tell it," I said, looking from him to my aunt. "She seems to be the only one who's trying here. And so far, she hasn't hidden anything from me. Right now, I trust her more than either of you."

Both of my parents were dumbstruck and didn't protest. Caroline took over the story.

"Shortly before you were born," she explained, "your father was arrested by the Evonian authorities and charged with espionage."

"Seriously?"

"It was beyond ridiculous," my father added under his breath. "I'd make a terrible spy."

"Well, my father didn't think it was ridiculous," said Caroline, still not looking at my dad. "He's the one who reported Miguel to the authorities."

"He only did that because he was trying to split us up," snapped my mom. "Which didn't work, by the way."

"Your mom fought to get me released from jail," my dad chimed in, trying to get the story back on track. "And I was."

"And then you promptly fled the country."
My aunt's voice was sizzling with bitterness.
"When you were just six weeks old, Grace,
your parents left and never returned. Not even
after your grandparents died."

"How could we bear to go back, after the
way Miguel was treated there?" my mom said
in a voice that was angry and tearful at the
same time.

The conversation tapered off, and I sat
back down, stunned. I tried to make sense of
it all—my grandfather accusing my dad of
spying, my dad getting arrested, my parents
fleeing my home country. It was a lot to
take in.

Finally, my aunt broke the silence. "I'd like
Grace to return to Evonia with me and be
officially introduced to society as the heir to
my title."

"What do you mean, your heir?" I asked.

"I have no children," Caroline told me, "so
when I die, you'll become the next Duchess of
Ardlan. So naturally, I'd like you to become
comfortable in Evonia."

My dad started to protest, but my mom put up her hand to stop him. She looked at me and asked, "Is that what you want?"

For a long moment, I didn't say anything. Ever since the divorce it had felt like my parents had been making decisions about my life without consulting me. I'd been angry about it. But now I truly didn't know what to do. This was so much to take in. Finally, I said, "I think I want to spend time with Caroline and see the country where I was born."

My dad gave me a small nod.

"Then it's settled," said Caroline matter-of-factly. "She can fly back with me by private plane tonight. I will return her in exactly three weeks."

I could see tears forming in my mom's eyes even as she nodded her approval.

6

Aunt Caroline sat in her air-conditioned car
making phone calls. My dad went back to his
house to get my passport. And my mom helped
me pack a suitcase. My mom was moving very
slowly and deliberately, as though she might
still be in shock from everything that had
just happened.

"What's the weather like in Evonia?" I
asked her as she took a dress out of my closet
and folded it carefully. I was trying to be
friendlier to her, already feeling bad about how
angry I had been.

"The weather is lovely in the summer. It isn't
hot and humid like this." She pulled a cardigan
that I never wear from the back of my closet.

Thinking about how much I didn't want to wear the cardigan, I threw my favorite blue hoodie into my suitcase and then another one too for good measure.

"Things at Caroline's home will be much more formal than you're used to," my mom said. "The ways we were taught to dress and eat and talk are very . . ."

"Royal?" I guessed.

"Refined," my mother said with a sigh. "My parents raised us as if we were always on stage. Caroline did well under that kind of pressure. I did not. I grew up feeling stifled by all the unwritten rules that we had to follow. I felt like I could never be myself." She hesitated for a moment and then added, "I wanted you to have a childhood where you felt free. You should be prepared for things to be different while you're visiting Caroline."

She finished folding a black dress that I had worn once to a funeral. "I wish I had time to take you shopping."

"I'm sure Aunt Caroline will take me," I replied.

"I'm sure she will." My mother laughed for the first time that day.

***

My parents walked me to the black SUV where Aunt Caroline and Duncan waited for me. I turned and hugged them before I got in.

"I'm sorry," my mom said, kissing my forehead. "I wasn't trying to keep secrets from you. It was just so hard on me and I didn't want you to have to deal with it."

I nodded. I wasn't quite ready to fully forgive her, but I also wasn't furious anymore. "Love you guys," I mumbled.

My dad handed me a list of numbers to call if, for any reason, I felt as though I wasn't allowed to leave. The US Embassy was listed at the top. Then he leaned into the SUV and said to my aunt, "Keep her safe. And promise me that she'll be back by August first."

My aunt just pursed her lips.

"Promise me." My dad's voice grew stern.

"You have my word, Miguel," Aunt Caroline said. I realized it was the first time she'd spoken to him, or even acknowledged his presence, since she'd gotten here.

I looked down at the slip of paper in my hands, and suddenly I felt a little scared about leaving home and going to the country my parents had run away from.

7

At the airport, a private plane was waiting for
us on the runway.

I looked around as I sat down in a leather
seat and was immediately offered an ice-cold
soda in a crystal glass. I'd flown on an airplane
once before, but it wasn't anything like this.

Dinner was served on fine china with real
silverware. And when I started to get sleepy,
I reclined my leather seat all the way back,
which turned it into a fairly comfortable bed.
I slept through the refueling in New York,
and when I woke, the sun was just rising.

My aunt was already up and having a cup
of tea. I was surprised by how nice she looked.
Her hair was freshly styled, and she was in new

clothes—a navy suit with a white silk scarf.

"Good morning," she said. "If you look out your window, you'll be able to see Evonia."

Outside jagged black cliffs rose from the sea along the green countryside below us. We flew over scattered little towns and descended to an airport just outside of a small city.

A car met us on the tarmac, and we drove through rolling hills. Eventually we reached an elaborate metal gate that marked the entrance to Caroline's property.

On the left side of the road, we passed a fenced pasture. A boy and girl my age stood with horses just beyond the white fence. They waved as we drove by.

"Who are they?" I asked.

"Sasha and Petra," my aunt said. "They help out at the stables. They're wonderful with the horses."

"My mom once told me she had a horse when she was a kid," I suddenly remembered. "We were driving through Iowa, and she pointed out a silver horse with a white mane standing in a field. She made my dad pull over so we could climb through a ditch and up to the fence to watch the horse."

"Yes, your mother and I used to go riding all the time," my aunt said. "She was quite good."

As we came over a hill, I saw what looked like a stone castle.

"Wow," I said. "Is this where you live?"

"Ardlan Manor," my aunt said. "It's belonged to our family for generations."

I pressed my forehead against the window as we pulled up. There were two towers on each end of the building and vines crawling up over the stone. It looked like something out of a fairy tale.

My aunt turned to me and said in almost a whisper, "You were born here."

"In this castle?" I asked, surprised.

"Yes," she said. "I remember that day like it was yesterday. I held you and you opened up your eyes and looked at me and gave this adorable little yawn."

I smiled. It was nice to learn about this after all these years. Maybe this place could feel like home in a way that Iowa never had.

8

Duncan introduced me to Ardlan Manor's staff. Duncan, it turned out, was not only my aunt's driver but also the manager of her household. He was in charge of the rest of the staff, my aunt's daily schedule, and all her social events.

My aunt looked at my astonishment with a gentle smile. "Duncan will help you with anything you might need."

"I actually do need something," I said sheepishly. "A toothbrush."

I'd forgotten one in my hurry to pack and hadn't realized it until I was on the airplane.

"You will find all the basic toiletries, including a toothbrush, in your bathroom," he said quickly.

"Thank you," I replied.

"Duncan is always one step ahead," my aunt said with an approving nod.

"I'll try not to be too much of a pain," I whispered to Duncan. He gave me a small smile.

Duncan led me up a flight of stairs and down a long hallway to my room. When I caught a glimpse of what was inside, I let out a small gasp of surprise. A massive canopy bed stood in the middle of the room, and there were several doors leading off to little side rooms and walk-in closets. One door led to a private bathroom with a staggering amount of marble surfaces. And, sure enough, I saw a toothbrush among the bottles and bars that were laid out on the counter.

Duncan looked pleased at my expression. He strolled across the room and opened a pair of doors that led out onto a balcony. A cool breeze floated into the room. I stepped out on the balcony and looked around.

"Could you take a picture of me?" I asked, handing Duncan my phone.

He looked a bit taken aback but agreed.

Once he'd handed me back my phone, I sent the picture to my parents to let them know I had arrived.

Duncan cleared his throat. "We will have visitors joining us for dinner tonight. They will be arriving at six."

"Tonight?" I said.

"Yes," he said. "Everyone is very excited to meet you."

"Me?" I had never been someone people were excited to meet before.

He just nodded at this and then cleared his throat.

"Before dinner, the duchess would prefer you remove the piece of jewelry attached to your nose."

"Umm, I can do that." I said, instinctively touching my nose ring.

Duncan gave a very quiet sigh of relief. "Very good," he said and then pointed to a landline phone beside my bed. "Dial zero if you need anything."

"Thanks, Duncan."

After he left, I turned to unpack my things, but as I sat down on my bed next to my suitcase, I realized how exhausted I was. I was jet-lagged, and the bed in my room was so soft. I climbed under the covers and was fast asleep almost instantly.

9

"Darling." My aunt shook my shoulder gently. "Our guests will be arriving soon."

I rubbed my eyes and sat up in bed. Outside, the sky had turned dark. A storm had rolled in.

"I just need to splash some water on my face, and I'll be right down," I said.

"You're going to need to change too." She eyed my rumpled clothes.

I looked down at my jeans and sweater and then started digging through my suitcase.

"How about this?" I asked, pulling out the black dress my mother had packed.

My aunt stared blankly at the dress, mouth slightly open. She composed herself quickly and said, "I'm sorry you had to pack in such a hurry. You probably didn't have a chance to pick out your best clothes. Go ahead and put that on and meet me out in the hall."

I blushed and didn't correct her assumption that I owned nicer clothes. After she left, I dressed and pulled on a pair of tennis shoes, fairly certain my aunt would appreciate this fashion choice about as much as she liked my dress. So not at all.

Out in the hall, my aunt looked at my feet and said, "But it's summer, my dear. Don't you have a pair of heels?"

I shook my head.

She sighed. "Follow me." She headed off down the long hallway. It was a good thing I was in a pair of sneakers rather than heels because there was no way I would have been able to keep up with her otherwise.

I followed her through a large wooden door that led into her bedroom. I stood awkwardly in the doorway as she disappeared into a huge walk-in closet that was even bigger than the one in my room.

"Let's see if these fit," she said, reappearing with a pair of black silk pumps. I slipped them on. They were a little tight, but they fit.

"Oh, much better," she said brightly. Then she disappeared into her closet again, this time returning with a black jewelry box in her hand. Opening it, she carefully took out a beautiful string of pearls with a sapphire pendant at the center.

"This used to belong to your grandmother, Lady Henrietta," she said as she took the necklace out.

The sparkling blue gem was more beautiful than anything I'd ever seen up close. And probably more expensive too.

I held up my hair as my aunt clasped it around my neck.

"And," Aunt Caroline said, reaching back into the jewelry box, "earrings to match."

I carefully clipped them on.

"Lovely," my aunt said, admiring me. "Now, we just need to do something about your hair."

And I let her pin up my hair. By the time I looked in the mirror, I didn't recognize myself.

10

My aunt told me to wait upstairs until the
guests arrived. "Once everyone is here, I'll
send Duncan to get you."

"So I'll be making a grand entrance?"
I asked.

"Of course. That is how the guest of honor
enters a room," she said with a smile.

So I went back to my room as my aunt
headed downstairs. I took dozens of pictures
of the view from the balcony and of my room
itself. Then I took a quick selfie.

Finally there was a knock on my door.
Duncan popped his head in my room and
gave me a nod. He led me to the stairs but
waited at the top.

"Aren't you coming?" I asked.

"It wouldn't be proper for a member of the staff to escort a young lady such as yourself," he said.

"That's weird," I said.

"It is proper etiquette," he said with a nod.

"Well, I'd feel more comfortable if I wasn't walking into that room alone," I responded with a hopeful smile.

"You'll be fine," he said in a slightly stiff way. Then, in more of a whisper, he added, "Walk tall. Chin up. Smile. Nod. And look everyone in the eye." He gave me another small smile, which made me feel a little bit better.

"Thank you," I said and then made my way down the stairs, happy when I made it to the last step without falling.

Four adults and three teenagers around my age were gathered at the bottom of the stairs waiting for my entrance. I understood right away why Caroline wanted me to dress up. The men, including a teen guy, were dressed in expensive-looking suits. And the women all wore cocktail dresses and pearls.

Everyone looked at me, sizing me up. I felt myself blush. I'd never been the center of attention—not like this.

"I'd like to introduce you to my lovely niece, Grace Valmont."

My aunt didn't use my full name. *Valmont-Diaz*, I wanted to correct her, but before I could say anything, Caroline started introducing the guests to me.

"This is Lord and Lady Middlebrook," she said, gesturing to one of the adult couples. "And their charming children, Lisle and Victor." Lisle was a platinum blonde girl my age, and Victor was a tall, dark-haired guy a year or two older.

I smiled at Lisle and then turned my attention to Victor. His eyes were the same color as the sapphire around my neck. They shined. I stuck out my hand to shake his, but when he took my hand in his, he raised it to his lips and kissed it.

That had never happened to me before. I felt a flush of heat in my cheeks and neck.

He lowered my hand and said, "Welcome

to Evonia. I hope you'll allow me to show you around."

"I'd love that," I said.

Then Lisle came forward and kissed me on the cheek, which completely threw me off. "So delighted that you're here," she chirped.

"And these are Lord and Lady Gilspead," added Caroline, moving right along. She nodded at the ginger-haired girl standing next to the Gilspeads. "And their daughter, Jaqueline."

Jaqueline smiled at me with a row of teeth that seemed too small for her mouth and leaned in to kiss me on the cheek, but I stuck out my hand to shake instead.

"So American," she said with a smirk.

"Now," said Caroline, "as the guest of honor, Grace, would you care to give a toast?"

A member of my aunt's staff appeared next to me and handed me a crystal goblet filled with sparkling water.

"Umm. Thanks for having me," was all I could think to say. I took a sip from the goblet, but my mouth still felt extremely dry.

11

After a few minutes, Duncan came out to announce that dinner was ready.

My aunt sat at the head of the table, and I sat to her right. Victor sat next to me. And the girls were at the other end of the table, whispering to each other.

I looked down at my place setting to see an alarming number of forks and spoons in front of me. I had no idea what they were each for, so I watched my aunt, who seemed to know I needed guidance and put her finger on the tiniest fork when the first course was served. Unfortunately for me, the first course was oysters. I had never been a fan of shellfish, so I just casually sipped at my water and hoped no one would notice that I wasn't eating.

"So," I said to Victor, "tell me something about this country that I don't know."

"Well," he said nodding to the grey slime in front of me. "Oysters are served at nearly every meal."

"Really?" I said. Then I lowered my voice. "I don't like them."

Victor laughed. "Not *really*, but they are quite common. If you douse them with lemon juice, they aren't so bad."

"Looks like it worked for you," I said, noticing that he had already eaten his portion.

He grinned. "Quick, no one is looking. Switch plates."

I gave him a grateful smile as we swapped. Nobody seemed to see—apart from my aunt, who was giving me a disapproving look that was easy enough to ignore.

"Thank you," I whispered.

"Maybe you'll learn to love them," he said with a smile.

"Maybe." I said. "If they're served deep-fried I might try them next time."

After that Victor and I chatted in an easy conversation about Evonia and the various dishes we were being served. I forgot about everyone else at the table and let myself relax.

12

After dinner, my aunt whispered to me, "The adults will be withdrawing to the parlor. I trust you can keep your peers entertained in the meantime."

This was not exactly welcome news. I had never been one of the popular kids who had lots of people over for parties. And so far tonight, I had only really talked to Victor, which meant I had no idea what to say to the girls.

Caroline didn't wait for me to respond, though. Which was starting to seem like a pattern, now that I thought about it.

Once the adults had left the dining room, Lisle and Jacqueline looked at me expectantly.

I cleared my throat. "So do you guys

want to . . ." I paused. I hadn't been here long enough to know what there was to do in the manor. "Go see my room?" I finished lamely.

But the others seemed content with that suggestion, so I led them up to my room. When we got there they immediately plunked down on some chairs as if they hung out here all the time.

Lisle looked around my room casually. Her eyes finally settled on me and she asked, "So what was it like growing up in America?"

I was taken aback by the question. "I don't know. Normal, I guess."

Jacqueline scrunched her face at my response. Victor smiled encouragingly and said, "Go on, tell us about it. What do people do in the States? Where do you live?"

I shrugged. "I live in a small town where nothing much happens." Victor still looked interested, but the girls didn't, so I added offhandedly, "Besides, I'm not sure I'm the best judge of what's typical in the States, since my mom grew up here and never quite adjusted to life in Iowa."

"Yes," Jacqueline said, perking up. "We've heard stories about your mother."

"What stories?" I said, sitting down on the last available chair.

"I'm sure they're just rumors," Lisle said with a smile. "But I heard that she was absolutely wild. A party girl. And that she dated a rock star!"

I smiled. "My dad was in a band for a couple of years, but they never got famous. Just a few opening gigs with bands on European tours."

"We've also heard—" Jacqueline started.

Lisle cut her off. "Don't say it."

"What?" I asked.

"Oh, it's just a rumor," said Lisle.

"Tell me," I said.

"Well, some people say your father kidnapped your mother," Jacqueline burst out, looking eager to hear more about it.

I laughed, then realized she was being at least somewhat serious. "Uh, sorry to disappoint you, but that's not what happened. My parents are actually really boring. They've even had a relatively boring divorce."

"They're divorced!?" Lisle said, clearly shocked.

"Yeah," I replied. Although I wasn't happy about their recent divorce, I had more than one friend with separated parents and it didn't seem *that* out of the ordinary.

"Why?" Lisle asked.

I shrugged. Their divorce still bugged me and I didn't really want to talk about it.

"All right, that's enough, Lisle," said Victor, giving his sister a stern look. "Let's do something."

"What should we do?" Lisle asked.

"Hide and seek?" Victor suggested. His mischievous grin made it perfectly clear that he wasn't thinking of an innocent kid's game.

Desperate for any excuse to get out from under the spotlight, I jumped up. "That's a great idea," I said. "Let's explore this place. I've barely had a chance to even look around."

"Not even the dungeon?" Victor asked.

"The what?" I said, startled.

"The dungeon," he said matter-of-factly. "All castles like this have one."

"How would you know?"

"Well, my mother is one of your aunt's best friends, so Lisle and I have spent a lot of time here over the years. We've explored this place from top to bottom, haven't we, Lisle?"

Lisle shrugged. "You have. I usually stay with Mother and Lady Caroline."

"I still can't believe there's an actual dungeon," I said.

Victor raised his eyebrows. "Let's go down there and I'll prove it to you."

Was there a flirty look in his eyes, or was I imagining it? Either way, I was curious. "Sure," I said. "Lead the way."

13

When Victor opened the door to the
dungeon, a damp, coppery smell rose up from
the darkness.

"We need a light," I said.

Victor pulled out his phone and tapped
on a light before starting down the stairs.
Formal cocktail attire does not include ideal
places to store a cell phone so I didn't have
mine with me. Glancing back at Jaqueline
and Lisle, I could see that they were phoneless
too. So we quickly followed Victor before
his light disappeared around a bend in
the staircase.

"I don't know about this," Jacqueline said
when we got to the dark passageway at the

bottom of the stairs. "There are probably rats down here."

"Or worse," Victor added cheerfully.

She froze. "I'm going back up," she said.

"What about you, sister dear?" Victor asked Lisle with a smirk.

"I'll kick any rat that I see," she replied defiantly.

I was impressed with Lisle. Maybe she and I would get along.

Jacqueline gave Lisle a pouty look, clearly upset at being left out, but bolted back up the stairs all the same. The three of us continued down a long hallway. Suddenly Lisle bumped into Victor and he dropped his phone with a loud *crack*. I jumped at the noise and the sudden darkness.

"Sorry! I've got it," Lisle said, squatting down to the ground in search of the phone. It only took her a few seconds to locate it and turn the light back on, but when she stood back up with it, Victor was gone.

"Where did he go?" Lisle asked, looking genuinely concerned.

"He couldn't have gone far," I said.

"Maybe he's—" Lisle started to say, but she was interrupted by a long, drawn-out moan.

"Victor?" I said, following the sound. But there was no answer. I walked down the hallway a little farther—just beyond the reach of the phone's light.

"BLAH!" Victor yelled as he jumped into my path.

We both jumped and then Lisle smacked Victor in the chest.

"You are horrible," she said. "Absolutely horrible."

Once the shock wore off, I couldn't help giggling. It was a dumb prank, but it had worked. There was something charming about Victor.

"But check this out," Victor said, pointing to the spot where he'd been hiding. In the dim light, it looked like some kind of old-school jail cell. "Can you imagine being imprisoned down here? It would be dark twenty-four hours a day."

"Oh, man, I hope my dad didn't get stuck

in a cell like this," I murmured, suddenly horrified.

"What do you mean?" Lisle said.

"Uh, well, he got arrested at one point. I guess my grandfather wasn't happy he married my mom," I said trying to make a joke out of something dark, something I hadn't totally wrapped my head around yet.

"I'm sure he wasn't kept down here," Victor said, reaching for my hand in the dark. "Or anywhere as old-fashioned as this."

"If he was," I said, "I totally understand why my parents fled the country after I was born."

"I'd flee too," Lisle said. "In fact, let's get out of here."

As she headed back toward the stairs, Victor kept holding my hand but didn't budge.

"Grace Valmont," Victor said, and I didn't correct him. "I'm glad you're here."

"I am too," I said.

"Do you mind if I kiss you?" Victor asked. The light from his phone seemed to make his eyes shine and sparkle even down in the dark passageway.

"Yes," I said.

"Yes, you mind?" he said.

"No," I said and then, "Yes." And then I just kissed him to make my point clear.

14

Victor and I climbed back up the stairs hand in hand, but just before we got to the door, he dropped my hand. When I saw the look on Jacqueline's face, I knew why.

As we headed back toward my room, I whispered to Lisle, "Are your brother and Jacqueline dating?"

"They're always off and on," she said, rolling her eyes. "They attend different boarding schools—Jacqueline in Paris, Victor in London—so every fall they break up and every holiday they get back together."

"Are they together now?"

Lisle smiled at me. "Why? Are you interested in him?"

But just then Duncan rounded a corner and I was saved from having to answer.

"There you are," he said. "I've had trouble tracking you down. Where have you been? Your parents would like to leave soon."

"Just playing a game of hide and seek," Victor replied innocently.

As we followed Duncan to the parlor, I noticed Jacqueline glaring at me.

"Jacqueline asked Victor to be her escort to the coming-out ball," Lisle whispered to me, continuing our conversation as though we hadn't been interrupted. "But that was before they got into a big fight last week."

"The *what* ball?" I said.

"The coming-out ball. All of the teenagers of noble families are introduced to society when they turn sixteen. You'll be there too."

"Uh, I'm not sure I'll be doing that," I said, stalling. My aunt never said anything about a ball. In fact, she hadn't gone into any detail about my responsibilities as a future duchess. And a fancy party didn't really sound appealing to me.

"Of course you will. It's the whole reason you're here, isn't it?"

"I guess," I said, though that *wasn't* why I came all the way over here. I came here to try to understand my past, to learn about everything my parents had kept from me.

"Your aunt has already told everyone you're going," Lisle said. "I know she's been plotting to get you here for the ball for years."

This surprised me. I'd thought my aunt had wanted to make up with her sister and get to know me. It bugged me that this whole trip was now about some society ball that I hadn't even agreed to attend.

In the parlor, while everyone got ready to leave, Victor took my hand and led me to a corner, out of everyone else's earshot.

"Will you go on a proper date with me?" he said.

"Aren't you dating Jacqueline?" I asked. "I don't want to cause any problems between you two." *And I don't want to start anything with a guy who's already in a relationship*, I added silently.

"No," he said. "Jacqueline and I have gone out in the past, but we're just friends now."

I waited for his eyes to meet mine, but he was looking past me toward the main hall.

"Really?" I wasn't convinced, especially since it seemed like he was looking at Jacqueline as he said it.

"Really," he said, and this time his blue eyes locked on mine.

"Well, in that case," I said, still cautious, "I'll think about it."

15

At lunch the next day, Aunt Caroline raved about how successful the previous night had been. "It seems like you were getting along well with the Gilspeads and the Middlebrooks."

I only nodded. I still felt a bit confused about where I fit in with the nobility. My aunt didn't seem to notice.

"Although there was that unfortunate incident with the oysters," she said absentmindedly. "But the entrance and the introductions went quite well, I thought. And it was good practice for you to get ready for the coming-out ball next week."

"What is this coming-out ball, anyway? You haven't really explained it to me."

"Oh, it's a tradition for Evonia's noble families. It's only a formality at this point. Just announcing your place in society really. But I couldn't let you miss it, regardless of what your mother and your foolish father think about making your own choices and being fully aware of—"

"So you were planning this all along?" I cut her off. My voice was sharp. "You lied to me about wanting to get to know me and make amends with my parents? It was all just a way to manipulate me into coming here so you could show me off to your society friends?"

"Well, it's not just for my benefit, Grace." My aunt gave me a stern look. "I know you haven't known about your heritage until recently, but you really need to start taking on Valmont family responsibilities."

"And what if I don't want them?" I was starting to understand why my mom had rejected this life.

The question caught Caroline off guard, but she didn't get a chance to respond.

Duncan entered the room, and I felt a flash of embarrassment, realizing that the entire household could probably hear our argument.

"What is it, Duncan?" Caroline asked a little snippily.

"I've received a call from the staff at the Middlebrook household," he said. "They've asked if it would be convenient for Victor to take Lady Grace horseback riding on Thursday at eleven."

"Why didn't Victor just call *me*?" I asked Duncan. He didn't seem to know what to say.

My aunt sighed, but she was smiling again. "This is the way that things are done, Grace," she said. "Victor Middlebrook comes from a very old, very distinguished family. He has excellent breeding." I wrinkled my nose at the word *breeding*, but Caroline was already turning back to Duncan. "Say that Grace will be delighted to accept."

"Hold on! I don't know how to ride," I said. But it was more than that. I was suddenly concerned that this was just another one of my aunt's manipulations.

"Not to worry," said Caroline. "Duncan can arrange for you to have some lessons down at our stables this afternoon." She stood up. "And now I must be off. I may or may not be back in time for dinner," she said on her way out the door.

I was stunned. We hadn't finished our conversation. She had completely ignored my concerns about this ball, shutting out any room for argument about that or the Valmont family responsibilities, as she called them. And now I would have to take riding lessons.

I grumbled but went upstairs to change into jeans and a T-shirt anyway.

As I pulled the shirt over my head, I spotted my phone sitting on the bedside table. I grabbed it, figuring I should send a message to my parents. I didn't know what to say, but I wanted to tell them at least something about what Aunt Caroline was trying to do.

Then I hesitated. I knew that my parents would be furious if they thought Caroline was taking advantage of me. And although I was no longer convinced that she really cared about making amends with my parents, I didn't want to give up on the idea that we could all be a family someday. So instead, slowly and deliberately, I typed out a message letting them know that I would be attending the coming-out ball.

My dad replied within seconds: *THE WHAT?!*

A message from my mom flashed across the screen: *Miguel, we will talk about this separately. If that's what you want to do, Grace, do it. But please don't let your aunt make you do something you aren't comfortable with.*

I sighed. I wasn't sure I was comfortable with attending a fancy ball, but I didn't want my parents to know that. So I typed a quick *yep* in reply and put my phone back down.

"They are ready for you at the stables whenever you want to go," Duncan announced when I came back downstairs. "Would you like me to drive you?"

"No thanks, I'll be fine," I said. From what I remembered, the stables were only about a mile down the road. I would have happily walked twice that far without a second thought. I only wished I had my skateboard with me.

Outside, the weather was perfect: not a cloud in the sky and a cool breeze blowing over the rolling green hills.

As I approached the stable, I heard music playing. To my surprise, I actually recognized the song from one of my dad's band's old albums.

I walked up to the stable and knocked on the wooden doorframe as I entered. Inside, in the stall just to my left, a boy with curly hair the color of wet sand was brushing a horse. Two stalls down, a girl with hair the same color hair waved to me.

"Good afternoon, Lady Grace," the girl said with a big smile on her face.

"Hi," I said awkwardly, looking around for the source of the music. Then I spotted a battered-looking MP3 player sitting on a bale of hay. "This song," I said. "How do you know it?"

"My favorite band," the boy said as he picked up the MP3 player and turned it off.

I was shocked, but all I could manage to say was, "Cool."

"I'm Sasha, and this is my sister Petra," he added.

"Yeah—nice to meet you. My aunt said you two can teach me how to ride."

"That we can," Sasha replied.

"Really, all you have to do is hold on. These horses are all super well trained," Petra added.

"I think Misty would be the perfect horse for her, don't you?" Sasha asked his sister.

"Oh, he would," she agreed. "I've already got him saddled up and ready to go."

Petra led a beautiful black horse out of the stable and showed me how to get up on his back.

"I'm going to walk beside you," Petra told me.

"The key to riding Misty is to keep loose reigns and to trust your instincts," Sasha said. "He's a good horse. When you feel comfortable, we'll go for a little ride."

They were right. Misty was a wonderful horse. I felt comfortable after just a few laps around the fenced-in pasture.

"Good boy," I said, rubbing his neck. "Good horse."

"Are you ready?" Sasha asked. "You seem like a natural."

"I'm ready," I said.

Once Sasha and Petra were mounted on their own horses, we headed toward one of the nearby hills.

Misty seemed to know the way. I barely had to direct him at all.

I couldn't help but think that it was much easier riding horses with Petra and Sasha than it was talking with Victor, Lisle, and Jacqueline.

16

After our ride, I helped Sasha and Petra wash the horses and brush their manes.

"You don't have to do this," Petra kept saying.

"I want to," I said. "Besides, there isn't really much else for me to do at the moment."

"We should show you around town," Sasha said.

"It isn't very big," Petra added. "But there are some nice little cafés, and we were planning to head into town tonight anyway."

"Perfect," I said. "That means I won't have to hang out by myself all night. Duncan doesn't necessarily seem like he'd be game to binge-watch shows with me."

Petra laughed. "Yeah, Duncan might not be up for it. But couldn't you at least call a friend or something?"

"Nah," I replied, "I haven't explained all of this Evonia stuff to my friends yet."

"Why not?" Sasha asked.

"Well," I said, "this is all super new to me. I had no idea I was even related to anyone royal until just a few days ago."

"Oh, that explains everything," Sasha laughed. "You weren't raised as royalty."

"Not even close," I said. "And I'm not sure how to share the news with people back home."

Sasha looked at me closely. "You know, it's probably easier to just tell everyone at once. People are going to find out eventually, right? At least if it comes from you, you can control the story."

I wasn't convinced. "I don't really feel in control of anything right now."

"Making an announcement might help with that," Sasha said with an encouraging smile. "People may try to use you once they find out you're royal, but I'd imagine it's pretty easy to spot if they are."

I hadn't even thought about that. I'd mostly been concerned that people back home would somehow use this weird development as another excuse to make fun of me. But Sasha had made a good point—some people might try to get on my good side when they found out my family was rich and important. I wasn't sure which one would be worse.

"It's totally up to you, obviously," said Sasha. "But it might be a relief just to put it out there. I think it's what I would do if I were in your shoes."

"Yeah, I'll think it over," I said.

I invited Sasha and Petra back to the house, but they both shook their heads with what appeared to be mild alarm.

"Meet us down here at five," Sasha said. "We'll be done with our work by then."

So I walked back alone. Duncan greeted me at the door to tell me my aunt would not, in fact, make it home for dinner and to ask what I would like to eat.

"Oh, don't worry about me," I said.
"I made plans to go to town with Sasha
and Petra."

"Oh," Duncan said, slightly surprised.

"I'll be home by nine," I told him.

"Yes," he said with a worried look on his
face. "It would be best for you to be home
before you are . . . missed."

I went up to my room and plopped down
on my bed, thinking of what Sasha had said.
I looked through my phone at all the photos
I had taken since I'd arrived. There were a lot
of pictures of my room and a few from the
beach this afternoon. When I came across
the selfie I had taken, I paused. It was a good
picture. And what did I have to hide, anyway?

Holding my breath, I pulled up my main
social media app and posted the picture on my
wall with the caption *suddenly royal*. Then I
quickly closed out of the app. I wasn't ready to
see the reaction yet. *Baby steps*, I told myself.

17

At a quarter to five, I walked back down to the stable, where Sasha and Petra were waiting with an old, beat-up car. Petra drove us into town.

At the cafe, I grabbed a table as Sasha and Petra ordered for us.

Bracing myself, I opened up my app again.

I had twenty new notifications and almost sixty new friend requests. I clicked on the notifications. Chrissy Swenson had commented on my photo. *Where are you? You look beautiful. That necklace!*

Sasha had been right about people's reactions. It was clear that the girl who'd taunted me for years wasn't genuinely interested in being my friend. She was just hoping to get closer to royalty.

I made a mental note to reject every new friend request that came my way in the immediate aftermath of the post.

Sasha and Petra sat down at the table with me and I put my phone away. I preferred talking to people that were actually interested in my personality, not just my status.

We ate the sandwiches that Sasha and Petra had ordered and talked until the café owner stepped onto the tiny stage. She announced that open mic was about to start and that anybody who wanted to perform should talk to her.

"Well, I guess that's me," Sasha said. He got up and walked over to the manager.

"He's going to perform?" I turned and asked Petra.

"Yeah, he plays guitar and sings. He's actually good too," she said with a shrug. "He regularly draws a crowd at the open mic nights here. I've told him he needs to get out of Evonia. Our country is so small. If he headed to America, he might get noticed over there."

Sasha suddenly appeared again holding a guitar.

"Where did that come from?" I asked him. "Do you just stash guitars everywhere you hang out?"

He laughed. "Nah, I had this one in the car. Just went out to grab it." He plucked the strings and soon had his guitar all tuned up. Then the owner gave him a nod and he stepped on stage.

Petra was right. He was good. More than a few of the people watching started singing along. He clearly was relatively popular here, if the locals knew his song lyrics.

After a few songs he joined us again at the table.

"You were great!" I told him. "Were those original songs?"

"Thanks," he smiled at me sheepishly. "Yeah, I write a bit."

"Would you like to play together some time?" I asked. I had never really played with anybody except my dad, but I liked the idea of playing music with Sasha.

"You play?" Sasha looked surprised.

I nodded.

"That'd be cool."

After a few more people finished their time on stage, the owner came up to us. "Sasha, do you feel like doing an encore? Nobody else is signed up and I'm hoping to keep the open mic going awhile longer."

Sasha shook his head but pointed to me. "Let's give other people a shot. My friend Grace can play."

I looked at him in alarm and shook my head.

He looked sheepish. "Sorry. I thought you said you played."

"I do. I just don't normally play in public." In fact, I had actually *never* played for an audience before—my parents didn't count.

"Well, now's your chance to try it! What's the worst that could happen? Nobody here knows you anyway." He lowered his voice and leaned close so the owner wouldn't hear him. "It's not like we're going to introduce you to everyone as Grace Valmont."

"Grace Valmont-Diaz," I corrected him instinctively. It felt good to set the record straight, even if it was just for Sasha.

He looked confused. "Diaz?"

"Yep," I said. "That's my dad's name."

"Oh." He looked thoughtful for a moment but then snapped out of it. "Well then, Grace Valmont-Diaz, care to give it a try?" He smiled encouragingly at me and handed me his guitar.

I couldn't deny that the idea was appealing—and the owner was staring at me with a desperate look. So I stood up and made my way to the stage.

Avoiding eye contact with everyone in the audience, I started strumming the last song my dad and I had been working on. I heard the chatter of the café die down and by the time I finished playing, everyone was looking up at me. But the only person I was looking at was Sasha. He beamed at me and joined in on the applause. My heart did a somersault.

18

The next morning my aunt showed up in my bedroom with two white shopping bags.

"You'll need riding clothes for your outing with Victor," she announced.

I looked at the tweed jacket, white blouse, black pants, velvet riding hat, and riding boots in the bags she had passed me.

All sorts of new clothes had appeared in my closet this morning too. Three new dresses. A blue blazer. A tweed skirt. And three pairs of shoes—all heels.

"Oh, you shouldn't have," I said hesitantly. The idea of wearing formal clothes while riding didn't seem appealing.

"The boots are new, of course, and the

helmet. But these were actually some of your mother's old riding clothes. I thought you might like them. The fashions have stayed pretty much the same."

I didn't care about the fashion, but I was shocked that my aunt had kept my mom's old things.

As if reading my mind, Aunt Caroline added, "I have such good memories of riding with your mother, I just couldn't get rid of those clothes."

I smiled at her. Maybe she really was trying to make an effort after all. In her own way. I hadn't thought of how lonely and horrible it must have been for her after her sister left and her parents died. Everything about her was always so put together—her beautiful clothes, her perfectly styled hair. But I realized that regardless of how perfect she *looked*, she never actually seemed that happy. Except maybe when she'd been reminiscing about the day I was born.

I hugged my aunt. "Thank you," I told her.

She blinked rapidly, as if she were forcing back tears. "I just want you to know," she

said, with a smile that revealed a dimple
I hadn't noticed before, "that you are my
favorite niece."

"I'm your only niece," I laughed, and she
laughed too.

"Family is a precious thing," she said.

I hugged her again, thinking about how
much we had both missed out on.

***

The riding clothes were comfortably broken
in, but the boots hurt my feet. Still, I didn't
complain when I came downstairs because both
Aunt Caroline and Victor were smiling at me.

"Victor," I said. "You're early."

"My apologies," he said. "I couldn't wait to
see you again."

My aunt beamed at me.

"You two have a wonderful day," she said.

Outside, Victor led me to a sporty white
convertible.

"Hop in," he said.

"We can just walk to the stables," I said. "It
isn't that far."

"We could," Victor said, holding the passenger open for me, "Or we could just drive."

Looking down at the stiff new boots on my feet, I caved.

"Nice car," I said as I got in and Victor started the engine.

"It is, isn't it?" Victor said with a grin. "A gift for getting top honors in school this year."

"Wow," I said. "I think I got, like, a strawberry ice cream cone for getting good grades this year."

"Imagine what your aunt would get you if you got good grades!"

"I bet she'd get me a pony."

"She totally would," Victor said.

We both laughed.

When we entered the stable, I saw that Sasha and Petra had two horses ready for us.

"Hey," I said to them. "You two should come riding with us."

Victor looked confused. "I'm sure they have work to do. We don't want to keep them from it."

"Yes," Sasha said. "Wouldn't want to do that." His tone was biting.

"You two have fun," Petra said, trying to lighten the mood.

Sasha helped lead Misty out of the stable.

"Remember," he said, staring at me intensely. "Trust your instincts."

"I will," I said, pulling myself up on the horse, swinging my leg over, and sitting up. "Always have."

Victor clicked his tongue at his horse, and instantly they were racing out of the paddock toward the hills.

"Come on," he called over his shoulder.

"Let's go," I said to Misty, who followed at a brisk trot.

We rode across a wooden bridge and through a small wooded area. Eventually we stopped near a clearing where there was a table set up. I saw a huge picnic basket sitting beside the table.

"A little lunch I had prepared for us," Victor explained as he hopped off his horse.

He helped me to the ground and then tied

our horses to a tree before sitting down at the table.

"This is amazing," I said as Victor opened the picnic basket. Inside there was a thermos filled with tea and two containers. One was filled with tiny sandwiches and the other with chocolate dipped strawberries.

"I tried to get us some deep-fried oysters, but those are really better fresh," he said with a grin.

I laughed.

It was a beautiful place for a picnic, and everything Victor packed was delicious. Once we started talking, the conversation just flowed. Victor started telling me all about his friends from boarding school. "And what about you? What are your friends in America like?"

I shifted uncomfortably. "I actually don't have that many friends. And the ones I have aren't *close* friends."

Victor smiled knowingly. "All that will change now," he said. "As soon as people know you're royalty, they'll start treating you differently."

I thought back to what Sasha had said about people who would want to befriend me only because of my family. It was amazing how different the two boys were.

"I have something that I want to ask you," I said, nervously avoiding his eyes.

"Ask me anything. I'm an open book."

"Why were you weird about Sasha and Petra coming along earlier? They're really cool. Petra is so nice and Sasha plays the guitar and . . ." I trailed off once I caught a glimpse of his face.

He looked a little irritated. "Well, I would have thought that was obvious. I wanted to go out with *you*. I didn't really want other people tagging along."

"Oh," I said, a little embarrassed that I didn't think of this myself.

"To be honest," he continued, his tone a little softer, "I didn't want to have to compete for your attention on our date."

He tilted his head and looked at me for a moment. "Can I kiss you?"

I nodded enthusiastically.

The kiss lasted for just a moment and then he looked at me again and said, "I'm sorry if you thought I was rude earlier. I wouldn't want you to think your escort to the ball was some kind of jerk."

"Escort?"

"Yes," he said. "If you'll have me. I'd love to be your date to the coming-out ball."

I remembered Lisle saying something about an escort, but I hadn't realized I would need a date for this event. Why did people keep springing this stuff on me? Still, I did like the idea of spending more time with Victor. "Uh, sure, sounds good to me. You never know when I might need someone to secretly eat oysters for me."

He grinned. "Grace, I like you. You're so honest and beautiful, and you make me laugh."

"Um, thanks," I said. I knew I should probably return the compliments, but in the end it was easier just to keep kissing him.

19

Back at the stables, I led Misty into his stall.

"I can take her," Petra said.

"I don't mind," I said, starting to brush out Misty's mane.

"Well," Victor said as Sasha walked into the stable carrying a bale of straw. "I need to get going. I have tennis lessons in an hour."

"Okay," I said. "You can go ahead. I'll walk back later."

"Grace," he said, glancing at Sasha. "It wouldn't be proper if I didn't bring my date back home. And maybe you'd like to join me for tennis lessons?"

I didn't really want to take tennis lessons, and I was surprised at his suddenly formal tone.

Petra looked at me. "Let me take care of Misty," she said and then whispered, "Go."

Victor stood in the doorway waiting for me.

"I'll be right there," I said and watched as Victor turned around and walked to the car.

I scratched Misty's ears and whispered a goodbye to the horse. But as I turned to go, I heard Sasha humming the tune to the song I'd played the night before.

I peeked my head into the stall he had disappeared into and saw Sasha spreading fresh straw on the ground, still humming.

He looked up with surprise as I had caught him humming. "It's been stuck in my head since last night," he told me.

"I guess we need a new song, then," I said.

"We do."

"Grace," I heard Victor calling. "We really should go."

"I'm not sure you'll have time," Sasha said, not looking me in the eye. "You seem pretty busy now."

"I always have time for music," I said. "Tomorrow?"

"Tomorrow," Sasha agreed. His brown eyes lit up and I noticed that they contained specks of gold.

I smiled at him and turned to head out of the stable.

Victor looked impatient as he leaned against his car waiting for me.

"What were you doing?" he asked.

"Just helping out," I said.

"You are such an American," he said, laughing in a way that felt almost cruel.

"What do you mean?" I said, getting in the car.

"You try and help with everything, even if it isn't something you should concern yourself with." He slammed his driver's side door shut with more force than was really necessary.

"You think I shouldn't concern myself with taking care of the horse when I'm done riding him?" I asked.

"That's not it," Victor said, rubbing his forehead. "I just mean that you're royal and you have staff to help you. It's the help's responsibility to—"

"They have names," I cut in. "Petra and Sasha. And I don't consider them *the help*, I consider them friends."

There was an awkward pause. "Look, I'm sorry," he said. "I didn't mean it like that. It's just, in Evonia, we have all these unwritten rules, especially for people with noble backgrounds."

"Well," I said. "I've always believed some rules need to be broken."

"I'm sure you do." He seemed to be really thinking about this and quietly drove his car away from the stables.

Victor smiled at me as we pulled up to the front of the manor. "Maybe it's about time that someone like you shook things up. I just hope . . ." he paused, as though he wanted to choose his next words very carefully. "I hope that nobody tries to take advantage of you and your willingness to help others."

I gave him a quizzical look as I stepped out of the car. *Why does everybody feel the need to give me advice about how to handle all of this new royalty stuff?* I thought.

I told him that I couldn't play tennis—that I had to do something with my aunt.

"Thank you for a beautiful lunch," I said as I got out of the car.

Victor opened his mouth to respond, but then his phone began to buzz. He pulled it out and seemed eager to answer it, so I gave him a little wave and turned to go inside. As I went up the front steps, I heard him say, "Good afternoon, Jaqueline," in a slightly snooty voice. "I'm on my way to my tennis lesson, so I'm afraid I can't really talk."

But when I got inside and looked out a front window, I saw that Victor was smiling as he drove away, the phone still pressed to his ear.

20

That evening, my aunt asked me to join her in the sitting room after dinner. "I thought you might enjoy looking at some old photo albums," she said as we sat on a sofa together. "This one is full of pictures of your mother and me from our coming-out balls."

I could tell we were both thinking about how our last conversation about the ball ended up.

But since it seemed like my aunt was trying to make an effort, I figured I should too. I sighed. "I'll go to the ball if that's what you would like, Aunt Caroline."

She beamed at me.

"But," I added, "I'd like to be introduced

as Grace Valmont-Diaz. I think it's important for people to recognize that I belong to both families. Even if Evonians have the wrong idea about my dad."

The smile on Aunt Caroline's face faltered for just a second. "I suppose I can live with that," she said with a short nod.

Together we paged through the pictures in the photo album.

"Do you still have your dress?" I asked.

"Yes," she said. "It's packed away somewhere."

"Is my mom's dress still here too?" I asked, looking at a photograph of my mom. Her gown was elegant and simple with no unnecessary frills.

"I think so. I'll have Duncan look for it." Then she smiled at me and said, "Tomorrow, a dozen dresses are being delivered from Paris. I know you'll find just the right one."

"Wow," I said. "Thank you."

But I wasn't confident that any dress flown in from Paris would be my style.

***

The next day the dresses arrived, and so did Lisle and Jacqueline. Aunt Caroline thought it would be fun for them to help me pick out a ball gown for the big event. She apparently hadn't picked up on the awkwardness between Jacqueline and me.

The girls sat at a table drinking tea while I went into my walk-in closet to try on the first gown. Two staff members had to help me into the gown and zip me up. The dress was heavy and scratchy, and I felt like a giant marshmallow. I didn't want anyone to see me in that dress, but the women helping kept telling me how beautiful I looked and hustled me out of the closet.

"Oh, turn around," Lisle said. "Give us a twirl."

I did, and the dress swirled around me.

"Now move around the room," Lisle directed. I did as she said and Jacqueline started to laugh.

"What?" I asked.

"Hasn't anyone taught you how to walk?" Jacqueline said. "Chin up. Shoulders back.

You act as if the dress is dragging you down."

"It weighs a ton," I pointed out, but Jacqueline still looked critical.

"And what are you wearing on your feet?" Lisle asked.

"Socks," I said.

"You need to wear heels," Jacqueline said.

"I don't have any," I said, lying.

Jacqueline looked at me in confusion. "That is the saddest thing I've ever heard."

Lisle stifled a giggle but then got up and came over to me.

"Here," she said and placed a book on my head. "Balance this as you walk."

I practiced walking around the room and Lisle pretended to be my escort, but the book kept falling and every time it slid from my head, Jacqueline laughed.

"So," Jacqueline said as I passed her, the book still on my head. "Is Victor going to be your escort?" She was clearly trying—and failing—to sound casual about the question.

The book fell from my head and landed on the floor with a thud.

"Look," Lisle said impatiently, turning to Jacqueline. "If he wants to go with Grace, let him go. She's going back to the States soon anyway."

"Where she belongs," I heard Jacqueline say under her breath.

I bent down to pick up the book. I wished I could just disappear. This was becoming almost unbearable. And to make the situation even more uncomfortable, I wasn't even sure how I felt about Victor. Or about how he felt about me. I thought back to how his face looked when he was on the phone with Jaqueline the other day.

"Oh my," my aunt said as she stepped into the room. "Look at you!"

"I feel like it's a bit much," I said. Then I quickly turned my back on the girls and headed for my walk-in closet. My aunt followed me.

"We'll find something," she told me with an encouraging smile. She helped me pick out the next dress to try on. Even though all I wanted was to put on my hoodie and a pair of jeans, I agreed.

I tried on all twelve dresses and they were all just as terrible as the first. I wanted a dress like the one my mother had worn for her ball, but everything I tried on was bedazzled or covered in mountains of lace. When my aunt asked which one was my favorite, I didn't know what to say. After a few awkward seconds I finally said, "They're all so different from what I'm used to. I can't decide."

"Don't worry," Aunt Caroline said. "You have a few days to think about it."

My aunt left to go to lunch with a friend, and I retreated to the closet to change into my normal clothes. Lisle poked her head in and said, "That first dress wasn't so bad. And my mother's seamstress can work miracles. I can send her over, and she'll tame the dress down."

"Thanks," I said, grateful for the offer.

Then I added in a hushed voice, "I think Victor should take Jacqueline. I don't want to create any trouble. Really, I don't."

"But he wants to take *you*," she said.

I didn't know how to tell her that I wasn't sure how *I* felt about it anymore, so I just said,

"Tell him it's okay to take Jacqueline. If he already promised to take her, he should. I don't mind going alone."

"You *can't* go alone. You just can't," she said.

"I could go with Sasha." I don't know what made me say it, but it just jumped out.

"Who?" Lisle said.

"Sasha," I repeated. It was too late to go back on it now, and besides I didn't really know anyone else. "He helps out in the stable."

Lisle looked horrified.

"Go with my brother," she said. "Don't worry about Jacqueline. She has a million boys who would love to be her escort."

"We need to get going, Lisle," Jacqueline called from outside the closet, cutting the conversation short.

As Lisle headed back to the table to gather up her things, Jacqueline came up to me and whispered, "No matter what you wear, you'll still never be true royalty. Your father took that away from you."

She turned and walked away before I could think of anything to say.

21

Even after the girls were gone I was still shaken a little bit from what Jacqueline had said. *How could anybody behave like that?* I thought to myself. *And why the heck didn't I defend myself?* I walked down to the stables as a distraction. I needed to get away from all that lace and silk and nobility for a while.

Petra and Sasha were feeding the horses. "Need any help?" I asked. They told me how much food to give each horse and taught me how to clean out the water troughs.

As we worked, I said impulsively, "Would you two like to come over for dinner tonight? My aunt will be away, and I hate the idea of eating all alone in that great big dining room."

"Oh, poor you," Sasha teased.

"Come on," I said. "Please."

And after much begging, the two of them agreed to join me up at the house that night.

***

When Petra and Sasha arrived I couldn't help but laugh. They were both dressed like they were going to a cocktail party. Sasha was wearing a tie and a suit jacket that was too small. Petra was wearing heels and a dress.

"You didn't need to dress up," I said, showing them to the dining room. "We're just having pizza."

"Whoa," Sasha said. "Pizza on china and with candlelight."

"Ordering the pizza itself was my first act of rebellion," I said. "I don't want to throw the manor into complete chaos."

After dinner, I took them both up to my room and showed Petra the racks of ball gowns. She admired each one.

"They're all so beautiful," she said, turning to me. "But none of them seem very . . . you."

"I know," I said, still thinking about my mother's dress. Suddenly I had an idea. For the first time since I had arrived at the manor, I walked over to the phone and dialed zero. I felt embarrassed doing it, but I wanted to know if Duncan had found the dress. He appeared moments later.

"Good evening, everyone," he said, nodding to each of us. "How can I be of service?"

"Did you find my mom's ball gown?" I asked.

"I did," he said. "I found both your mother's and your aunt's. They are airing out right now."

"Do you think I could try on my mom's dress?" I asked.

Duncan smiled. "I will bring it right up."

He left and reappeared carrying a garment bag much smaller than the ones that had contained the dresses I tried on earlier. I thanked him, grabbed the bag, and headed for the walk-in closet. Slipping on my mom's dress felt perfect. I took a deep breath before stepping out to model it for Sasha and Petra.

"That's the one," Petra said, beaming.

Sasha didn't say anything. He just stared at me.

"What do you think?" I asked him.

"I think you look great," he finally said.

I blushed and knew in that moment why I'd told Lisle that Sasha should be my escort, not Victor.

22

I changed out of the dress and when I walked back into my room, Petra and Sasha looked up in surprise and stopped talking immediately.

Petra excused herself to go to the bathroom, and Sasha and I looked at each other for a moment.

"I have something to ask you," I said to him.

He cleared his throat nervously. "Me first, okay?"

I nodded. "Go ahead."

He looked at me for a minute and then burst out, "Is your dad Miguel Diaz?"

I blinked in surprise. "Uh, yeah."

"The famous musician?"

"I don't know about famous, but you have his album, yeah. I heard you play it the first time we met."

"I knew it! I've been wondering about it ever since you mentioned your last name."

His strange look at the open mic night made sense now.

"Your dad was incredible. Does he still play?"

"A few songs here and there. But he doesn't perform, not anymore."

"I'd really like to meet him. Will he be coming here?"

"Ah, no," I said. "He didn't have the best experience over here."

"Well, I'm really hoping to go to America, but I'd need a work visa. Maybe your dad still knows some people in the business? I'm willing to intern or do all the grunt work at a record label or anything to do with music. You could let him know I'm a hard worker and then maybe he could hook me up with some people in the music scene . . ."

He trailed off as I looked at him.

"Sure," I said, my heart sinking. "I guess I can call him tomorrow."

"That would be incredible!" Sasha looked relieved. "Now, what was it that you wanted to ask me?"

Victor's prediction about people trying to take advantage of me for being nice was ringing in my ears. I just would never have imagined that kind of behavior from Sasha. "Nothing. Never mind." I gave Sasha a weak smile just as Petra returned from the bathroom.

"Did you ask her?" she said to Sasha.

"I did," he said, grinning.

"Oh, thank you," Petra said to me, without even waiting to hear what my answer had been. "Sasha wants to go to America so badly! He doesn't have any chance of being noticed in Evonia, but I know he can make a music career there."

She turned to Sasha and added, "And then you could be closer to Courtney again."

Courtney? Who is Courtney?

My stomach did a sickening flip. Not only was Sasha using me to get connected with my dad, but he had a girlfriend.

"Do you want to join us for a ride tomorrow?" Petra said as they got up to leave.

I swallowed back the bitter taste in my throat. "I think I might have plans."

23

For the rest of the week I spent a lot of time
in my room, avoiding both Victor and Sasha.
I passed on my dad's contact information to
Sasha and texted with Victor a little about the
arrangements for the ball, but that was it. My
aunt came by a few times to help me decide
on details for the night of the ball. How we
should do my hair. My makeup. What shoes
I should wear. I tried to go with the simplest
versions of everything she offered and for the
most part she agreed, although she did manage
to convince me to wear an old Valmont family
pin in my hair.

At one point, when she was showing me
the dozens of pairs of shoes she'd had sent to

the manor, she asked, "And have you decided on an escort?"

I sighed. "I guess it'll be Victor."

Aunt Caroline looked at me, her expression soft and understanding. "My dear, if you don't want to go with Victor, I'm sure we can arrange something else."

"No, I'll take Victor. It's fine." I was pretty confident that I didn't like Victor as more than a friend, and that he didn't really like me as much as he liked Jacqueline, even if he wouldn't admit it. But I just wanted to be done with these ridiculous ball arrangements in the easiest way possible.

My aunt stared at me and I avoided her gaze. "You know, I never did thank you for agreeing to all this," she said in a quiet voice. "I understand that this is a lot to take in and that it isn't for everyone. Your mother didn't like it. I don't think I realized how miserable this life made her until she met your father and I saw her completely happy."

I couldn't hold back the tears in my eyes, and when I looked up I saw that neither could Aunt Caroline.

"I should've mended things with your parents a long time ago," she whispered. "And I'm grateful you're giving me a chance to start. Life's too short to stay angry at the people you love." Then she kissed me on the forehead and left the room.

***

The night of the ball, I stood on the front steps of the house with Aunt Caroline, waiting for Duncan to bring the car around for us.

"I'm glad you chose that dress," Caroline told me. "It really suits you."

"Thanks," I said. At this point, I just wanted to get this whole thing over with. Then I could go home, where I was just ordinary Grace. Being a nobody again sounded very appealing after all I had been through over the past couple of weeks.

A limousine pulled up in front of the house. I walked down the front steps toward the car as the driver got out to open my door. Suddenly I froze, surprised that the driver wasn't Duncan.

"Sasha," I said, "I didn't know you would be here."

"Duncan said to tell you he's feeling a little under the weather tonight," said Sasha. "He asked me to fill in for him as your driver."

"Well, thank you for stepping in on such short notice, Sasha," said Caroline. "Go on, Grace, get in the car. It'll take us half an hour to get to Alaborn, and we don't want to be late."

"You look wonderful!" Sasha told me as I climbed into the backseat.

I blurted out, "So do you."

He smiled at this. So did my aunt.

24

At the royal palace, before the ceremony
began, Caroline and I joined about a dozen
other girls and their mothers. We were in
a private sitting room with a lot of mirrors.
Lisle and Jacqueline came over to greet me.

"Oh," Lisle said when I took off the white
cloak that was covering my dress. "Where
did you find that dress? I don't remember you
trying it on."

"It was my mom's," I said.

"Ah, a *used* dress," Jacqueline said.
"Of course."

"Vintage," I corrected her. "A vintage dress
from a time when people had style."

As I walked away from her, I suddenly

missed my mom and I wished she was there to see me in her dress.

Lisle caught up with me. "Sorry about Jaqueline," she whispered. "She's having a bad night. Her escort got sick at the last minute and can't come. She's going to have to go to the ball by herself."

I sighed. I was sick of Jacqueline's rudeness and pretty much over Lisle constantly defending it. I just turned away from Lisle, making up my mind that I wasn't going to let it happen anymore.

Just then, there was a knock on the door and the fathers came in to present their daughters with gifts.

I watched as Lisle's dad gave her diamond earrings and Jacqueline's dad handed her an emerald pendant.

"I have a special gift for you," my aunt whispered. "Just wait."

A moment later two more people came into the room: my dad and mom. "You guys!" I squealed, running over to hug them. "What are you doing here?"

"I paid for them to fly out," explained Caroline.

"And they won't arrest you again?" I asked my dad, half joking, half serious.

"Never again," my Aunt Caroline said. "I thought that if you were being presented as a Valmont-Diaz, it was about time Evonia got used to the Diaz part." She turned to my parents. "You are both always welcome. I'm so glad you've returned."

Aunt Caroline and my mom hugged each other and then both dabbed at their eyes at the same time, in the same way.

My dad came over to me. He held up a guitar case.

"Caroline told me I was supposed to give you a gift."

He set it on a table and I opened it. Inside was his old guitar—the one he had first taught me to play on.

"Thank you," I said, hugging him. "It's perfect."

25

When our escorts came into the room, I immediately noticed how Jacqueline looked at Victor. Suddenly I felt bad for her. Even though she'd been petty about it, it seemed like she really did like Victor. More than I did, at least.

"Victor," I said.

"What?" he said in a slightly alarmed voice. He'd been looking at Jacqueline in pretty much the same way she was looking at him.

"I don't like you," I said. Then, realizing how harsh it sounded, I added, "romantically. I don't like you the way you and Jacqueline like each other."

He opened his mouth to protest, but I held up my hand to stop him. "It's okay that you like her. I'm not offended. You two have history."

He hung his head. "To be honest," he mumbled, "I'm not really over her."

"Then you should be with her," I told him. "Her escort backed out."

"I can't," he said. "I made a promise to you."

"But you made a promise to her first," I said. "Do the right thing. Offer to be her escort again."

"What about you?" He said.

"I'll be fine," I said. "My dad is here. And my mom. I don't need anyone else."

I watched Victor sheepishly make his way over to Jacqueline. At first she ignored him, but eventually she smiled and took the hand he was offering her.

My parents were still talking to Caroline, so I sneaked out of the room without anyone noticing. I wanted to get some fresh air and be by myself for a few minutes.

I walked across the lawn, and in the distance I saw Sasha leaning against a tree. I walked toward him.

"What are you doing?" he said when he saw me approach. "Why aren't you inside?"

"Why aren't *you*?" I asked.

"I can't go inside," he said a little bitterly. "I'm hired help."

"You can come if you're my guest," I argued. "And, if you didn't already have a girlfriend, I would've invited you to be my escort."

"Girlfriend?" He laughed. "Since when do I have a girlfriend?"

"Courtney," I said. "Petra mentioned her."

"Courtney is a boy," he laughed again. "My best friend. We started a band together a few years ago. He's the drummer. That's why I wanted to get to the States. I wanted to introduce you to him. I had this vision of the three of us being in a band together."

For a moment I was too shocked to react. And then I burst out laughing.

"It's not funny," Sasha said with a serious look on his face. "I really think we could make it big."

"Let's take this one step at a time, Rock Star," I said. "I'm guessing this means you weren't trying to get close to me just so you could meet my dad?"

"What? No! Why would you think that?"

"Maybe because you asked me to connect you with him?"

"I was just excited because I thought he could help us get a band off the ground. But even before I realized who he was, I knew I wanted to work with you. And . . . spend time with you in general."

I smiled. "Will you be my escort tonight?"

"What about Victor?" He asked.

"He made a promise to someone else," I said. "Come on, walk down those stairs with me."

"I smell like horse," Sasha said with a laugh.

"I like the smell of horses," I said.

"Future band name?" He grinned. "The Smell of Horses?"

"Umm, no," I said, smiling.

Then I took his hand and led him inside.

SUDDENLY ROYAL

**THE VALMONTS ARE NOT YOUR
TYPICAL ROYAL FAMILY.**

MASON FALLS MYSTERIES

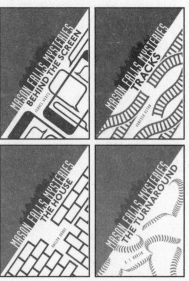

EVEN AN ORDINARY TOWN HAS ITS SECRETS.

K. R. COLEMAN is a writer, teacher, and parent of two boys. She has written half a dozen books for Darby Creek. Some of her favorites are *Deadman Anchor*, *Showdown*, *Truth or Dare*, and *The Freshman*. Under her real name, Karlyn Coleman, she has published short stories and a picture book entitled *Where Are All the Minnesotans?* Currently, she is working on a young adult novel entitled *Air*.